It was almost halftime. The score read Wildcats 3, Rockets 2. This time, the Rockets took possession of the ball. Brandon dribbled toward Aaron and the goal. Suddenly, Ricky charged out after him and tackled the ball so hard that Brandon fell flat on his face. He jumped up immediately, and before Ricky had a chance to clear the ball out of his territory, Brandon jumped on Ricky and threw him to the ground. Aaron rushed out of the goal to help Ricky, but two other Rockets players grabbed Aaron and pushed him down.

Other members from both teams joined in the fight. T.J., watching from the other end of the field, could hardly believe it. He couldn't see Ricky, and that worried him. His sturdy Mexican friend had gone down under a pile of Rockets. Was he all right, or was he broken and bleeding under that pile?

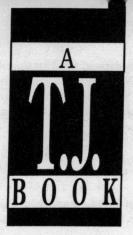

HERO
FOR A SEASON

NANCY SIMPSON LEVENE

Chariot Books™
David C. Cook Publishing Co.

Chariot Books™ is an imprint of Chariot Family Publishing
Cook Communications Ministries, Elgin, Illinois 60120
Cook Communications Ministries, Paris, Ontario
Kingsway Communications, Eastbourne, England

HERO FOR A SEASON

Scripture is quoted from The Living Bible, © 1971, Tyndale House
Publishers, Wheaton, IL 60187. Used by permission.

First Printing, 1994
Printed in the United States of America
98 97 96 95 94   5 4 3 2

Library of Congress Cataloging-in-Publication Data
Levene, Nancy S., 1949-
Hero for a season / Nancy Simpson Levene.
        p.   cm.
Summary: Nine-year-old T.J. receives God's help in unexpected ways
when he collects cans to recycle for cash to help his soccer teammate
Ricky Rodriquez and his family, who are experiencing both bad luck
and discrimination.
ISBN 0-7814-0702-8
[1. Moneymaking projects—Fiction. 2. Mexican Americans—Fiction.
3. Prejudices—Fiction. 4. Soccer—Fiction. 5. Christian life—Fiction.]
I. Title.
PZ7.L5724Can   1994
[Fic]—dc20

                                                        93-21126
                                                        CIP
                                                        AC

To Jesus,
who takes our smallest efforts
and multiplies them into
mighty miracles!
and
To Sandy Heyse,
a good friend and soccer buddy.

. . . [H]e took the five loaves and two fish, looked up into the sky and asked God's blessing on the meal, then broke the loaves apart and gave them to the disciples to place before the people. And everyone ate until full! And when the scraps were picked up afterwards, there were twelve basketfuls left over! (About 5,000 men were in the crowd that day, besides all the women and children.)

Matthew 14:19-21

ACKNOWLEDGMENTS

Thank you, Cara, for your interest and support, and thank You, Jesus, for making this book possible.

CONTENTS

1

FULLBACK TROUBLE

The soccer ball sailed high through the air and bounced a few yards in front of the goal. Almost immediately, the forward caught up to it and pushed the ball diagonally toward the big open net.

T.J. gasped! The other team was about to score! Suddenly, as if out of nowhere, a fullback for T.J.'s team roared into action. He charged toward the forward and made a clean tackle. Taking the ball away, the fullback kicked mightily and cleared the ball out of his territory.

SHREEEE! The referee's whistle blew, ending the game. The Wildcats defeated the Hornets, six to five. The fullback had saved the game for his team.

T.J. and his teammates cheered. It was the first game of the season, and they had beaten their most fierce competitors.

"Way to go, Ricky!" T.J. congratulated Ricky Rodriquez, their team's star fullback. Ricky's real name was Ricardo, but everyone called him "Ricky."

"You saved our lives on that last play," T.J. added.

"Thanks, T.J.," Ricky grinned as he trotted off the field. "You did pretty well yourself, scoring two goals."

"Aw," T.J. was a little embarrassed by the attention, but he was thrilled to have made them. Scoring against the Hornets was not easy.

"Good game, T.J.! Good game, Ricky!" said their coach, Mr. McLagan. The coach was from Scotland and had come to Kansas City to coach amateur soccer. T.J. grinned as he heard Mr. McLagan's Scottish accent mingle with Ricky's Spanish accent. Their team was getting international.

Mr. McLagan clapped Ricky on the shoulders. "I'm sure glad you stopped that forward from getting any closer to the goal," he said to Ricky.

"Yeah, me too!" exclaimed Aaron, the goal-keeper. He wiped imaginary sweat from his forehead.

They all laughed.

"Come on, T.J.! Your dad says to hurry. We gotta drive over to Charley's game," shouted T.J.'s best friend, Zack, as he ran up to them.

"Oh, yeah, I forgot," T.J. sighed. He hurried with Zack to his family's minivan.

"Jump in," T.J.'s father told T.J. and Zack. "Charley's game has already started." T.J.'s seven-year-old brother, Charley, was playing in the eight-and-under league this fall, while T.J. and his team had moved up to the ten-and-under division.

"You boys played very well today," T.J.'s father commented as they headed for yet another soccer field. "Together you scored all but one of the goals for your team!"

"Yeah!" T.J. and Zack grinned and slapped their hands together.

"Coach McLagan says we have the best front line in the league," T.J. proudly told his father.

"You have the best defense, too," Father reminded them. "Ricky Rodriquez played a spectacular game."

"Yeah, I'm glad we have Ricky on the team this year," replied T.J.

"We're sure to win first place in the division," Zack bragged.

"Don't be too sure," Father frowned. "This is an older division. You will be playing against ten year olds now."

"Aw, we'll beat 'em anyway," the two nine year olds said confidently. After all, the Wildcats had just defeated the Hornets. They were unbeatable!

Upon arriving at the field, T.J., Zack, and

Father joined Mother and T.J.'s little sisters, Megan and Elizabeth. They all stood on the sidelines and cheered as Charley's seven-year-old team made a brave stand against a team of eight year olds.

"Don't worry about losing," T.J. told his younger brother after the game. "That usually happens when you first start playing in these leagues. Just try and do your best. Next year, you'll be the older team and you can beat the other teams easy. That's what our team did last year. We came in first place."

"And that's what we're gonna do this year too," said Zack, "even if we have to play ten year olds."

"Right," agreed T.J. "We have you, me, Aaron, and Ricky. How can we lose?"

The following Monday at school, however, T.J.'s hopes for the team were nearly shattered.

"I have to drop off the team," Ricky Rodriquez sadly told T.J., Zack, and Aaron. The boys were at morning recess and had just begun to kick a ball around the blacktop area.

"WHAT?" the boys all cried in alarm. They stopped their play and gathered around Ricky.

"My dad lost his job yesterday," Ricky tried to explain. "He says that now we don't have enough money for food, let alone the soccer team. He says he can't afford to buy the gasoline to drive

out to the soccer fields."

T.J. stared at Ricky in disbelief. Ricky's dad had lost his job? He could not afford to drive to the soccer fields? T.J. remembered seeing Ricky's dad at the game. He seemed like a kind man. He smiled a lot. He had gotten quite excited at the game and called out to Ricky in Spanish. In fact, Ricky's whole family had come.

"But you can't quit," Zack's voice suddenly shook T.J. out of his thoughts. "We need you!"

"I can't help it," Ricky shook his head sadly.

"But the team won't be the same without you, Ricky," Aaron, the goalkeeper, complained. "I gotta have you blocking all those shots on goal."

"There's nothing I can do about it," Ricky threw up his hands in frustration.

"Well, there's something I can do about it," T.J. suddenly joined the conversation. "We can drive you to all the games. I know my parents won't mind."

"That's a great idea," Zack and Aaron agreed.

"I don't know," Ricky frowned. "My dad might not like that. He doesn't want people to have to do things for him. Besides, he doesn't want anyone to know he's out of work. I guess he feels embarrassed or something."

"But it's not his fault," T.J. objected. "Lots of people are losing their jobs now."

"Yeah," agreed Aaron and Zack.

"But you don't know my dad," Ricky insisted. "He doesn't want anyone feeling sorry for him or doing him any favors."

"Gosh, he'd be doing us a favor if he'd let you stay on the team," replied T.J. "We'll walk home with you after school and ask him if it'd be all right if we drive you to the games."

"Well, I don't know . . ." Ricky hesitated.

"Aw, come on," the boys persisted. "He can't refuse all of us."

"Well, okay," Ricky's face brightened. "Maybe it would work after all."

"That's the spirit," T.J. clapped him on the back. "Never say die!"

After school, T.J. called his mother on the telephone from the school office. He asked her if he could go to Ricky's house with Zack and Aaron.

"My mom says it's okay," T.J. told the boys a minute later. "She also said that you can ride with us to the soccer games," he told Ricky. "She said the team would be in bad shape without you."

Ricky smiled.

"Then let's go!" Zack and Aaron cried. They had already called their mothers and had permission to go.

The boys crossed the street in front of the school and started down a street in the opposite direction from T.J.'s house. Ricky's younger brother, Paulo, and younger sisters, Victoria and Alicia, walked with them.

They crossed another street, walked up a steep hill, and then started down the other side. "See, there's my house," Ricky pointed. "It's the blue and white one at the bottom of the hill."

"You mean the one with the rope swing?" T.J. asked excitedly.

"Yeah," Ricky nodded.

The boys walked ahead eagerly. In the front

yard of the blue and white house stood a great old tree. A rope swing with a wooden seat hung from its limbs. Several children played in the yard, taking turns on the swing.

"Are all those kids in your family too?" Aaron gasped. The yard seemed full of dark-haired children, all resembling one another.

"No," Ricky laughed at Aaron's shocked face. "Most of them are my cousins. They live across the street."

At that moment, Ricky's father appeared in the front yard. He waved to Ricky and his friends, then sat down on the front steps to watch the children.

"Can we try the swing?" Zack asked Ricky.

"Sure," Ricky replied.

The boys ran the rest of the way. They had almost reached Ricky's front yard when suddenly, a noisy car caught their attention. It turned onto the street and was speeding down the hill, making loud popping noises. Black smoke spewed from its tail pipe.

As the car sped toward them, one of the small children playing in the yard ran toward the street after a ball. "STOP!" someone cried, but the little boy kept on going. It looked as if he were going to run right out in front of the car. "HEY! LOOK OUT!" T.J. yelled as loud as he could.

2

A MEAN NEIGHBOR

Without stopping to think, T.J. rushed as fast as he could toward the little boy. He caught up with him an instant before he darted into the street. T.J. dove and tackled him. He and the boy rolled backward onto the soft grass just inches away from the street. The noisy car sped past them and on down the street.

For a moment, T.J. did not move. He lay in the grass, still holding tightly to the little boy.

"Whew, T.J., that was a close one!" exclaimed his friends, coming to stand beside him.

Ricky's father rushed over to T.J. and the little boy. He hugged both of them.

"Thank you for saving my little son, Miguel," Ricky's father told T.J.

T.J. was embarrassed. "Aw, it was nothing."

Ricky's father smiled. He invited the boys to come inside the house. They went into the kitchen where the boys sat at the kitchen table. The rest of the family pulled up chairs to join them. Several grown-ups and a number of children all crowded into the kitchen. Ricky's mother served the boys a plateful of cookies.

"Mmmmmm," the boys murmured as they bit into the cookies. They were the best sugar cookies T.J. had ever eaten. A distinct cinnamon flavor ran through them.

"These are delicious!" the boys exclaimed.

Ricky translated what they had said to his mother. She spoke only Spanish.

"Gracias," she replied.

"My mother's cookies were famous in Mexico," Ricky told the boys. "Now, they will be famous here in America."

"I can see why they are famous," Aaron declared. He reached for his third cookie. "They are great!"

This time, Ricky's father translated. Everyone in the kitchen laughed.

"It was nice that you boys could come home with Ricky," his father said. "We do not have many visitors."

"Oh, uh, thanks," T.J. replied. He suddenly remembered why they had come. "We think Ricky is the greatest defender we've ever had on our soccer team."

"Yeah," the other boys nodded their heads.

Ricky's father looked pleased.

T.J. plucked up his courage. "We came to ask you a favor," he told Ricky's father.

"I will do anything for you," his father answered. "You saved my little Miguel today." He hugged the three-year-old boy who sat on his lap.

T.J. looked at Ricky. His father sounded encouraging. Ricky motioned for T.J. to continue.

"I was wondering if you would let Ricky stay on the soccer team and ride to the soccer games with me? I already asked my mom and she said it was okay," T.J. said all in a rush. He waited breathlessly for Ricky's father to reply. So did everyone else. The room was silent.

Ricky's father stared at T.J. for a moment. Then he said, "I could not ask your parents to do this for Ricky. I do not have money to pay for the gasoline."

"That doesn't matter," T.J. insisted. "We have to drive to the games anyway. We have plenty of room in our van. Please let him come. You would be doing our team a favor."

"Please, Dad," Ricky put in. "I'd like to play soccer with my new friends."

Ricky's father hesitated. He looked at the anxious faces of all four boys. Finally he smiled. "Okay," he said and threw up his hands.

"YIPPEE!" the boys shouted. They ate another round of cookies to celebrate.

After the cookies were gone, the boys decided to try the rope swing that hung from the giant tree in Ricky's front yard.

"Hey, this is cool!" Aaron shouted. He ran full speed from the front door to the swing and leapt feetfirst onto it. He stood on the swing and soared as high as he could go.

"Aaron! Let somebody else have a turn!" Zack finally called.

"Okay, okay," Aaron let the swing slow down. Zack hopped onto the swing. He sat on it and pumped hard with his legs until he was flying high. He was happy to soar like that for a while, letting the swing carry him high above the lower branches of the tree. Finally, he let the swing slow down. He stood on the swing and rode it to a stop.

"Hey, that was great!" Zack told Ricky. "I wish I had one of these in my yard."

"My turn," T.J. announced. He jumped on the swing and pumped it high.

The boys all had a great time on the swing. They tried swinging double, with two boys facing each other, one boy's legs on top of the other's. They even managed to swing with three of them on the swing at once. But when they tried

swinging four at once, it was a complete disaster.

"Help, get off!" Aaron gasped. Being the biggest, he was on the bottom of the pile. "I'm getting squished!" he yelled.

Zack and T.J. could only laugh. They were sitting on top of Aaron. Their legs were tangled together so that they couldn't move. Ricky, who had been trying to climb on top of them, got his foot caught in the ropes. He practically hung off the swing by one leg. They finally had to call for Ricky's father to untangle them.

The boys were recovering from their episode, when suddenly, a ball of mud sailed through the air and landed SPLAT! at their feet. Looking up, T.J saw a boy glaring at them from the middle of the street. T.J. recognized him as a boy who attended Kingswood Elementary School, but he was at least a year older than T.J. and his friends.

"Dirty Mexican!" the boy yelled. "GO HOME!"

Ricky's father strode out into the yard toward the boy. He turned and fled down the street.

"What was that all about?" T.J. asked Ricky.

An angry scowl covered Ricky's face. "That boy is our next-door neighbor, Brandon Long," he replied. "His family doesn't like us. They call us names. I'd like to bust them one!" Ricky kicked violently at the swing.

"Now, now," his father grabbed hold of Ricky to calm him down. "I know it makes you angry, but we must try to get along with our neighbors."

"How can we get along with them?" Ricky asked. "They never even gave us a chance. They hated us from the first day we moved in here."

"I don't get it," T.J. scratched his head. "Why do they hate you so much?"

Ricky's father sighed, "They hate us because we are from Mexico."

"But that's no reason to hate anybody!" T.J. exclaimed.

T.J.'s friends agreed. "I think it's neat that you're

from Mexico," Zack told Ricky and his father. "I like knowing people from another country."

"Me, too," Aaron said. "And I already know two good things about people from Mexico."

"What's that?" the others asked.

"They bake famous cookies and they are top-notch soccer players!" answered Aaron.

They all laughed.

That evening, after dinner had been eaten and the other children had left the table, T.J. remained in the dining room with his parents. They were talking about T.J.'s visit to Ricky's house.

"I am so proud of you for saving Ricky's little brother from the car," Mother told T.J. for the third time.

"Aw, Mom, it was the only thing to do. I couldn't just let him run out into the street in front of the car, could I?" T.J. asked. "I wonder if the driver of that car was a creepy neighbor who doesn't like Mexican people."

"Oh, surely not!" Mother exclaimed. "Do you think someone would deliberately try to run over a little boy because they're prejudiced?"

"Maybe," T.J. answered. "The boy who threw the mud ball at us sure looked mean."

"Prejudice is a terrible thing," said Father. "It

can make people do things they wouldn't dream of doing otherwise. God made everyone in the world. No one is any better than anyone else. We need to treat everyone equally whether they are man or woman, whether they have dark skin or light skin, or whether they are from our country or another country."

"Right," T.J. agreed. "I feel sorry for Ricky. The neighbors are mean and now his dad is out of work. That's gotta be really hard. They have a lot of people to feed in that family."

"How many people are there in the family?" asked Mother.

"Well, I'm not really sure," T.J. frowned. "I know there's at least five children, but there are also other adults besides his parents. Ricky's grandparents live with them too."

"That is a lot of people to feed," Mother nodded.

"Yeah, and they're really nice too," said T.J. "Out of all the adults, only Ricky's dad speaks English, but everyone else smiled and laughed a lot."

"Well, I'm glad you thought to ask us to take Ricky to the soccer games," Father said. "That will help them out."

"I wish I could do more," T.J. replied. "I'd like to do something to help out the whole family. But I don't know what I could do. I don't have a job for his dad or a bunch of money to give them. I guess a kid like me can't really do anything big to help."

"Oh, I wouldn't say that," Mother told T.J. "You have friendship to give. People need friends to help pull them through the hard times. You are also giving Ricky a ride to the soccer games so he can stay on the team. I'm sure that makes him feel better."

"Yeah, but you and Dad are the ones who will drive him back and forth to the games," T.J. pointed out. "You pay for the gasoline. It's really your gift to Ricky."

"We wouldn't be doing it if it weren't for you," Father told him. "It was your idea. Mom and I wouldn't even have known about Ricky's need for a ride if you hadn't told us."

"I know, I know," T.J. frowned. "I'd just like to do something bigger to help out. It's horrible to see a neat family like Ricky's in trouble."

"Well, maybe you'll think of something else you can do," said Mother.

"Maybe," said T.J.

No one said another word, for at that moment, a loud crash sounded from the kitchen.

BANG! CRASH! BOOM!

"HELP!" someone cried. "HELP!"

3

A GREEN VOLCANO

T.J., Mother, and Father jumped up from the table and ran into the kitchen. What they saw made them gasp in alarm.

T.J.'s younger brother, Charley, stood on his knees on the kitchen counter, his arms raised above his head. He was reaching inside a kitchen cabinet, holding onto one of the shelves. The shelf was tipped dangerously, and most of its contents had spilled onto the counter and the floor below. White powder covered Charley's arms and shoulders. Red liquid dripped from the counter to the floor, mixing with more of the white powder to form a sticky pink goop.

"HELP! THE SHELF IS FALLING!" Charley shouted to his parents.

Father quickly rushed over to Charley. He reached into the cabinet and took hold of the shelf. With one hand he steadied the shelf. With the other hand he removed the remaining items off of it and onto the counter below. Father pulled the shelf out of the cabinet and inspected it.

"You broke off one of the corner posts that held the shelf in place," Father told Charley. "How in the world did you do that?"

"I don't know," Charley hung his head. "I just leaned on it."

"Charley, what is the meaning of all this?" Mother demanded. She was looking at the bottle of red liquid that had spilled to the floor.

"Red food coloring!" she exclaimed. "My floor is covered with red food coloring!"

"Sorry," Charley mumbled.

"I think you'd better start explaining what you are doing, young man," Father told his youngest son. But before Charley could say a word, Father's arm accidentally bumped into an open bottle that sat close to the edge of the counter. WHAM! The bottle crashed to the floor, spilling a clear but strong-smelling liquid.

"What's that smell?" T.J. cried, holding his nose.

"Vinegar!" both Father and Mother shouted. They grabbed for the bottle of vinegar at the same time and bumped into each other. Mother slipped and fell, landing in a puddle of vinegar, red food coloring, and sticky pink goop.

"OH, YUCK!" Mother cried. She stared at the splotches of red that covered her once-white slacks.

"Oh, boy, are you going to get it now!" T.J. told his brother.

"Charley!" Father exclaimed. "What is going on here? How did you make all this mess?"

Charley, now sitting on the kitchen counter, stared down at his feet. "I was making a volcano," he whispered.

"What?" Father asked. "Speak louder, Charley. For a minute, I thought you said you were making a volcano."

"That is what I said," Charley spoke up. "I was making a volcano."

Father and Mother stared at one another. T.J. burst out laughing.

"You were making a volcano?" Father asked, not believing what he had heard.

"Yes," Charley answered. "My teacher made one today at school. I asked her how to do it and she wrote the recipe down for me on paper. See, here it is."

Charley handed a piece of paper to his parents. T.J. looked at it too. At the top were the words, "Volcano Recipe." A list of ingredients lined the left side of the sheet. Mother, Father, and T.J. scanned the list of ingredients. Vinegar was there, and so was baking soda. It was the box of baking soda that had been turned upside down, spilling its powder everywhere. The baking soda had mixed with the red food coloring to form the sticky pink goop.

"I don't see red food coloring on the list," Mother frowned at Charley.

"That was my addition," Charley explained. "I thought it would be neat to have a red volcano."

Father and Mother looked at one another and shook their heads. T.J. chuckled. Charley was always performing some kind of scientific experiment and getting in trouble for it. T.J. remembered last fall when Charley was studying the behavior of grasshoppers. He had filled a box with grasshoppers and brought it inside the house. Somehow they got loose, and the house had been filled with the bouncy insects.

Another time, Charley was studying centrifugal force. He had balanced plastic dinosaurs on the blades of the fan that hung above the dining room table. At dinner, Charley turned on the fan and the dinosaurs fell PLOP! into everyone's dinner.

But this time, T.J. thought to himself, was the best. He looked at the broken cabinet shelf, the mess on the counter, the mess on the floor, and

Mother's red-stained slacks.

"Charley, I think your volcano has already erupted in my kitchen," Mother told her youngest son, "and you had better clean up this mess before I erupt!" Mother left the kitchen to change her clothes.

Father and T.J. helped Charley clean up the mess on the floor and countertop. When they finished, Father said to Charley, "From now on, you are not to run a science experiment by yourself. You are first to tell your mother or me. Do you understand?"

"Yes," said Charley meekly.

"Okay," Father smiled and rubbed his hands together. "Now, let's make a volcano!"

"All right!" T.J. and Charley cried together.

Father read the recipe while T.J. and Charley gathered the ingredients together.

"Mix one cup of water, 3/4 cup of vinegar, and 1/2 cup of dishwashing liquid in a bowl," Father told the boys.

T.J. measured out the water and dishwashing liquid. He let Charley measure the vinegar.

"Can we put in some red food coloring?" Charley asked his father as he stirred the mixture in a large mixing bowl. "A red volcano would look much better than a clear one."

"All of the red food coloring was spilled. It is on your Mother's slacks," Father reminded him.

"How about green?" T.J. suggested. "I can see green food coloring in the cabinet."

"A green volcano?" Charley exclaimed loudly. "Whoever heard of a green volcano?"

"So . . . we'll make the first one in history," T.J. said.

"Okay," Charley liked that idea. "Can we, Dad?"

"Okay, okay," Father laughed. "Be careful and only use a drop or two of the green food coloring. If we spill the green like you spilled the red, your mother might throw all of us out of the house."

"Throw you out of the house for what?" Mother suddenly appeared in the kitchen doorway, startling all three of them.

After they had explained, Mother herself dripped a few drops of the green food coloring into the volcano mixture. It turned a leafy green color.

"Neat!" cried T.J. and Charley.

"The next thing the recipe says we need is an empty twelve-ounce juice can," Father told them.

"But I don't have a twelve-ounce juice can," Mother replied. "I don't buy juice in that size container."

"Then what do we use?" Father asked.

"I know!" T.J. cried. He ran to the garage and came back carrying an empty soda pop can that he had gotten out of the box of cans to be recycled. "Let's use one of these," he suggested.

"Good idea," said Father. He cut off the top of the can with a can opener. "Now, we're supposed to put 1/4 cup baking soda into the can," he said.

The boys carefully measured the baking soda and poured it into the can.

"Then we put the can into a dishpan and build a mound of sand around the can," Father continued to read. "The can is supposed to represent a crack in the earth. In a real volcano, gas and steam build up under the earth and force liquid rock to erupt out of the crack. In our miniature volcano, if we pour a little of the green liquid into the can with the baking soda, it will produce a gas like the gas that forms under the earth. Then, our volcano will erupt just like a real one."

"Awesome!" exclaimed the boys. They went outside to collect a bucket of sand from the sandbox.

Back in the kitchen, the boys watched as Father stuck the soda pop can with the baking soda in the center of a dishpan. Charley and T.J. packed sand around the can. When they finished, the box and can looked just like a miniature volcano.

"This is neat," T.J. commented. "I wish my teacher had done this in first grade."

"Wait 'til you see it erupt," Charley told his older brother importantly. "It'll really be neat then!"

Father gave Charley a big soup ladle so that he could easily dip it into the bowl of green liquid and then pour the liquid into the can with the baking soda.

"Are we all ready?" Father asked in a loud voice. "The Fairbanks volcano is about to erupt!"

"Wait a minute! We're coming!" Mother called from another room. She had gone to get Megan and Elizabeth. They ran into the room and gathered around the volcano.

Charley, enjoying his important role in the experiment, slowly filled the ladle with green liquid. He then poured it into the soda can.

Instantly, the liquid began to bubble and fizz. It rose quickly up the can and spilled out of it onto the mound of sand surrounding the can.

"Wow!" everyone exclaimed. They clapped their hands and watched as the liquid bubbled, swirled, fizzed, and foamed. Charley continued to add the green liquid to the can until the bowl was empty and the sand around the can was covered with green "lava."

"Pretty cool," T.J. decided after the experiment was over. The rest of the family agreed.

"Charley, I have to hand it to you," said Mother, hugging her youngest son. "Even though you caused a disaster, you made a wonderful volcano!"

Everyone laughed.

"Well, at least we know one thing," T.J. said. "We are the first to have a green volcano."

"That's right," agreed Mother. "I think I like it better than a red one. It's more original."

"Can we take a picture of it?" Charley asked. "We might never have another green volcano."

"I think that's a good idea," laughed Father. "This is an event we will not forget for a long time."

"Amen," Mother added.

Father got the camera and took a picture of the volcano with all the children and Mother in the background. They then took apart the volcano and cleaned up the table.

T.J. washed off the soda pop can. He carried it to the garage and returned it to the box of cans ready to be recycled. As he dropped the can into the box, T.J. suddenly had an idea. He raced back to the kitchen at full speed.

"Hey, I got a great idea!" he announced to his parents. "I know a way I can help Ricky's family!"

"How?" both Mother and Father asked at once.

"Cans! Aluminum cans!" T.J. replied excitedly. "I can collect soda pop cans and recycle them and give the money to Ricky's family."

"That's a wonderful idea," Father said.

"I think so too," nodded Mother. "You can have all of our cans for starters."

"Great!" T.J. cried. "And I'll get Zack and Aaron to help too. I gotta go call 'em right away."

"Wait a minute," Father stopped him. "It's past bedtime. You'll have to tell them tomorrow at school."

T.J. lay awake for a long time that night planning the best way to collect aluminum cans. He decided to go door to door in the neighborhood and ask for cans. He could use his wagon to haul them, and his dog, a sturdy German shepherd named Sergeant, could pull the wagon. Zack and Aaron could help too. Oh, it would be a great thing to do for Ricky's family. T.J. pictured himself handing a large sum of money to Ricky's father. He pictured the happy faces of the Rodriquez family as they counted the money.

If only I could do it, T.J. thought. *If only I could make enough money to really help them.* To do such a thing, he knew he would need all the help he could get. He decided to ask the one person who could make it all possible. T.J. sat up in bed. He bowed his head and prayed, "Dear Lord Jesus, please help me to collect cans and make enough money to help Ricky's family. I pray in Your name. Amen."

Lying back in bed, T.J. fell asleep immediately. With God on his side, how could he fail?

4

TRAPPED!

On the way to school the next morning, T.J. told Zack and Aaron all about his plan to recycle aluminum cans and give the money to Ricky's family.

"Awesome!" Zack and Aaron cried. "When do we start?"

"Right after school," T.J. said excitedly. "I'll bring my wagon, and Sergeant can pull it."

"I can bring my wagon and my dog, Ranger, too" said Zack. Ranger was a good-natured golden retriever.

"I'll get my brother's wagon," said Aaron, "and I'll bring my dog, Zsa Zsa."

"Zsa Zsa!" Zack and T.J. exclaimed. "Are you kidding?" The two boys began to laugh. Zsa Zsa belonged to Aaron's mother. She was a large white poodle, always neatly trimmed. Aaron's mother dressed Zsa Zsa in brightly colored sweaters, usually pink and purple. It was always funny to see Aaron, the Wildcats husky goalkeeper, out for a walk with Zsa Zsa, the fancy poodle.

"What's so funny?" Aaron said. "Zsa Zsa's big enough to pull a wagon."

T.J. and Zack stared at one another. "You mean we gotta walk around with a poodle in a pink and purple sweater?" they asked.

Aaron grinned. "I'll tell you what," he said. "I'll tell Mom to put Zsa Zsa in her raincoat. It's royal blue and is decorated with Kansas City Royals baseball designs."

"Oh, no!" T.J. and Zack laughed even harder. Zack fell to the ground and held his stomach. T.J. doubled over with laughter.

"I know what's the matter with you guys," Aaron teased. "You're jealous. You're just afraid that Zsa Zsa will outshine your dogs. Don't worry, I'll tell Mom to leave off Zsa Zsa's rhinestone collar." With that, Aaron stuck his nose in the air and strutted on up the sidewalk.

T.J. and Zack followed, laughing hilariously. It looked like they would be spending the afternoon with a German shepherd, a golden retriever, and a fancy white poodle!

When the boys reached school, they hurried through the halls to get to their class. As they rounded a corner, they met up with none other than Brandon Long, Ricky's next-door neighbor.

"Well, if it isn't the Mexican lovers!" Brandon snarled.

"Ricky and his family are great people!" T.J. replied hotly. "Quit calling them names!"

"Yeah, they're human beings just like you!" cried Zack.

"Is that so?" Brandon scowled. "I say they're nothing but dirt!"

The boys did not reply, for at that moment a teacher stepped out of her class and into the hallway. She frowned at Brandon. The older boy moved away quickly.

"I can't believe how stupid some people can be," T.J. muttered to his friends.

"When you listen to someone as prejudiced as Brandon, it makes you want to be extra nice to someone like Ricky," decided Aaron.

The other boys agreed. They continued on down the hallway to their third-grade class.

The morning passed quickly for T.J.'s class. Their teacher, Mrs. Tuttle, led the students in an arithmetic lesson and then held various reading groups. T.J., Zack, Aaron, and Ricky practiced their soccer skills at morning recess. Back in the classroom, they copied spelling words over and over.

Soon, it was time for lunch. Mrs. Tuttle told the class to line up at the door. The boys rushed to the end of the line. They liked to be at the back so that they could act silly and clown around. It was a game they played to see how funny they could act without Mrs. Tuttle catching them. They had done pretty well so far this year, although Mrs. Tuttle had once caught T.J. walking down the hallway on his hands and feet like a monkey.

Today T.J., Zack, Aaron, and Ricky were busy walking in circles and panting like dogs when Aaron suddenly grabbed T.J. by the arm and pointed to a door in the hallway.

"Hey, if you want aluminum cans, you oughta go into the teachers' lounge," Aaron told T.J. "They have a pop machine in there, and there's always a bunch of cans sitting around the room."

"Really?" T.J. asked.

"Yeah, I know. I've helped Mrs. Tuttle get supplies out of there before," Aaron said importantly. "There's a big supply closet in the back of the room."

"Gee, do you think we ought to go in there?" TJ hesitated. "It's really only for teachers, you know."

"Aw, come on," Aaron waved his hand. "What's collecting a few cans gonna hurt?"

The two boys ducked into the doorway of the teachers' lounge. No one noticed them, not even Zack, who was still in line and too busy turning circles with Ricky.

Aaron turned the doorknob. The door opened, and the boys cautiously peeked inside. There was no one in the room. They quickly slipped inside and closed the door behind them.

"Wow!" T.J. exclaimed. Aaron was right. Empty soda pop cans sat at various angles on a big table in the center of the room. At one side of the room was a refrigerator, pop machine, and candy bar machine. On the other side was a microwave and a sink.

"This is neat!" T.J. cried. "I wish we could have soda pop and candy bars for lunch."

"Yeah, teachers get all the breaks," sighed Aaron.

"What's back here?" T.J. wandered into a large open closet. Various boxes were stacked high on shelves. Giant boxes sat on the floor. T.J. looked at one of them.

"Wow, here's a box almost as tall as me, and it's full of paper towels," T.J. told Aaron.

"Yeah, this is the big supply closet I was telling you about," Aaron said. "It has just about everything in it you'd ever need."

The boys looked at a few more boxes. Then T.J. said, "Maybe we oughta get the cans and get out of here. We could get in trouble if Mrs. Tuttle notices that we're gone."

"Yeah," Aaron agreed. "We can use one of these empty boxes to carry the cans." He picked up a medium-sized empty box.

"Good idea," said T.J.

The boys started back into the lounge area when loud voices suddenly sounded at the door. They stared in alarm as the doorknob turned and the door slowly opened.

"Quick! Hide!" Aaron hissed. He grabbed T.J., and the two boys dove behind the giant box of paper towels a second before the door burst open. A flood of teachers filled the lounge. They called to one another in loud voices.

"Hey, Sally! What's for lunch today?"

"The usual—salad and diet soda."

"Does the microwave work? I need to heat my soup."

"John, are you really going to eat that big piece of cake?"

"Does anybody know if the microwave works?"

T.J. and Aaron sat in the darkened supply closet behind the big box of paper towels and listened to the teachers' conversation. It sounded

so funny that they had to cover their mouths with their hands to keep from laughing. They didn't want the teachers to catch them hiding in the closet. If that happened, they would be in all kinds of trouble!

Time went by. Some teachers left the lounge while others arrived. The boys were reminded of their own lunch period. It was surely over by now. T.J.'s stomach began to grumble. So did Aaron's. The boys became restless. What were they going to do? They had missed lunch and now they were missing recess. Soon, it would be time to go back to the classroom. Their teacher would miss them.

They would get into trouble. The more T.J. thought about it, the more he wished he had never stepped foot inside the teachers' lounge.

Then something happened that let T.J. know they had been missed and were already in trouble. A new teacher suddenly arrived in the lounge. As soon as she began to speak, T.J.'s heart sank. He silently groaned and looked at Aaron. The teacher was none other than Mrs. Tuttle. She spoke excitedly to the other teachers in the lounge.

"I can only stay long enough to eat this sandwich," Mrs. Tuttle said. "A terrible thing has happened. Two boys from my class are missing!"

"What?" cried the other teachers.

"Yes! We can't find them anywhere!" Mrs. Tuttle went on. "I know they were with the class when we started for the lunchroom, but it seems they never got there. No one can find them. Their friends have no idea where they went. It's as if they disappeared!"

"Oh, dear!" another teacher exclaimed. "What are you going to do?"

"Well, Mrs. Larson said that if we don't find them soon, we'll have to call their parents and the police!"

Back in the supply closet, T.J. and Aaron

looked at each other fearfully. Not only did the principal, Mrs. Larson, know they were gone, but she said she might call the police! They were in for it now. They knew they should come out of hiding, but they were too afraid to do so.

"What should we do?" T.J. whispered to Aaron.

"I don't know," Aaron whispered back. "I think we've really had it."

"Maybe we oughta just stand up and let Mrs. Tuttle know we're here," suggested T.J.

"In front of all the teachers in the lounge?" Aaron hissed. "Are you crazy?"

"But you heard what she just said. If we don't come out of here soon, they're gonna call our parents and the police!" T.J. replied loudly, a little too loudly.

"Shhh," Aaron quickly clamped his hand over T.J.'s mouth, but it was too late. Someone had heard them.

"Did you hear that?" one of the teachers in the lounge asked. "I thought I heard something back there in the closet."

"So did I," another teacher agreed. "I am sure I heard what sounded like whispering!"

T.J. and Aaron held their breath and scooched down behind the box of paper towels as far as they could. Chairs scraped the floor as the teachers got up from the table. Footsteps sounded as they moved into the closet area. A closet light was snapped on. T.J. ducked his head and prayed to become invisible.

His prayer was not answered.

A voice suddenly spoke right above T.J.'s head. "Well, hello, boys! You can come out now."

T.J. slowly raised his head and looked up into the stern face of Mr. Carpenter, the fourth-grade teacher at Kingswood Elementary School. Mr. Carpenter reached his hand out to pull T.J. and Aaron up from behind the giant box of paper towels.

"I believe there is someone here who will be very glad to see you," Mr. Carpenter said to the boys as he turned to Mrs. Tuttle.

"Oh, my goodness!" Mrs. Tuttle exclaimed when she saw T.J. and Aaron. "You mean you boys have been hiding in here all this time? Why would you do such a thing?"

T.J. and Aaron opened their mouths to try to explain what had happened, but before they could say a word, the door to the lounge burst open. Mrs. Larson, the school principal, stood in the doorway. Behind her, in full uniform and looking very grim, was a police officer!

5

THE FIGHT

Mrs. Larson and the police officer stared at T.J. and Aaron. T.J. wished he could somehow drop through a hole in the floor and disappear.

The principal, Mrs. Larson, was the first to speak. "I see we have found the missing boys."

"Yes," Mrs. Tuttle answered. "We found them just this moment. They have been hiding in the supply closet all this time."

"In the supply closet!" exclaimed Mrs. Larson. "T.J. and Aaron! I can hardly believe you boys would do such a thing."

"I'm sorry," T.J. whispered. He stared at the floor. He did not dare to look at Mrs. Larson. Although he tried to stop them, tears stung his eyes. He quickly wiped them on the sleeve of his shirt. T.J. could hear his friend Aaron sniffle beside him. Being in trouble with the school principal and the police was serious.

"Let's all go to my office," Mrs. Larson suggested. T.J. and Aaron followed the principal down the hallway while the police officer and Mrs. Tuttle walked behind them. T.J. felt like he was under arrest. He wouldn't have been surprised if the police officer was holding a gun behind them.

"Suppose you boys tell us what this is all about," said Mrs. Larson as soon as everyone was seated in her office.

T.J. exchanged a quick glance with Aaron. There was silence. Finally, T.J. spoke. "We went to the supply closet to get some cans."

"Some cans?" Mrs. Larson looked puzzled. "Cans of what?"

"He means empty soda pop cans," Aaron explained. "We are collecting them to help Ricky's family."

"Ricky who?" Mrs. Larson still looked confused.

"Ricky Rodriquez," T.J. said, feeling a little braver. "His father lost his job, and I got this idea to collect aluminum cans and recycle them and give the money to Ricky's family."

"That's a very nice idea, T.J.," Mrs. Larson said, "but what does that have to do with hiding in the supply closet?"

"Well, we went into the teachers' lounge to get the empty cans," Aaron tried to explain further, "but I guess we got scared when teachers started coming in for lunch. So we hid in the supply closet."

"I see," the principal stared at the boys and tapped her foot. A prolonged silence filled the room. Finally the police officer broke it.

"May I speak to the boys?" he asked Mrs. Larson.

"Why, certainly," Mrs. Larson replied.

"Do you boys play sports?" the police officer asked T.J. and Aaron.

"Sure," T.J. answered. He was surprised by the question. "We're on the same soccer team. I'm a forward and Aaron's the goalkeeper."

"Then you know that when you play any kind of sports, you must play by the rules or you get penalized," said the police officer. "Isn't that right?"

"Yeah," agreed T.J. and Aaron.

"Well, it's the same way with life," the police officer told them. "No matter what you do, you must go by the rules. If you are driving a car, you must obey the traffic laws. If you go to the grocery store, you must stand in line, wait your turn, and then pay the right amount of money. You see, there are rules for everything, and just like in sports, if you don't follow the rules, you must pay the penalty."

"Hmmmm," T.J. frowned. He hadn't really thought about that before.

"You boys broke the rules when you went into the teachers' lounge without permission and hid in the supply closet," said the police officer.

"Yeah, but we were doing it for Ricky and his family," T.J. pointed out. "Doesn't that make a difference?"

"No, not really," replied the officer. "Having a good reason does not make it right to break the rules. Let's put it this way. If you are playing soccer and you foul someone while trying to score a goal, should your goal count?"

"No," the boys answered quickly.

"Why not?" the police officer wanted to know. "Isn't making a goal a good thing to do?"

"Yeah, but you can't commit a foul while you're scoring a goal," said T.J.

"Why?" persisted the police officer.

"Because it's against the rules," cried T.J.

"Exactly!" the officer smiled. "Even if you're doing something good, you still have to follow the rules. If you break the rules, sooner or later, you have to pay the penalty."

T.J. and Aaron looked at one another and sighed. They wondered what penalty they would have to pay for hiding in the supply closet.

As if in answer to their thoughts, Mrs. Larson said, "I'm going to have to call your parents and tell them what happened today. I'm also going to ask Mrs. Tuttle to keep you inside during recesses for the rest of the week. That is your penalty for committing a big foul at school today."

T.J. sighed again. He was really in trouble now. Oh, why had he done such a stupid thing? He had known it was wrong from the beginning. Why did he let himself get talked into doing things he knew were wrong?

T.J. stood up with Aaron, and they both followed Mrs. Tuttle out of Mrs. Larson's office and down the hall to the cafeteria. They were allowed to eat a quick lunch before returning to the classroom.

All afternoon, T.J. had trouble concentrating on his studies. He wondered when Mrs. Larson would call his parents and what they would say. He dreaded the end of the day when he would have to face them.

When T.J. got home from school, Mother sent him to his room immediately. They only talked briefly. But when Father got home from work, he and Mother climbed the two flights of stairs to T.J.'s bedroom.

"Do you want to tell us what happened at school today?" Father asked T.J. as soon as he and Mother found seats on the lower bunk of T.J.'s bunk bed.

T.J. told his parents everything that had happened, including the police officer's talk about doing things the right way and following the rules.

"We agree with that," Father said after T.J. had finished speaking. "It's important to follow the rules and do things the right way."

"I know," said T.J. "It wasn't like I started out to do something wrong. It just all sort of happened. I don't know why I do things that I know are wrong."

"We all do that," Mother said to T.J. "It's because we are human beings and are not perfect. When we go to live in heaven, then we will be perfect and do everything right."

"Well, I'm gonna try and do things right from now on," T.J. declared. "I'm gonna choose the right way instead of the wrong way."

"Good for you," said Father. "I'm sure that if you ask Him, your heavenly Father will help you."

"Good idea," T.J. agreed. Right then, he bowed his head and prayed, "Dear God, please help me to always do the right thing and to stay out of trouble. I pray in the name of Jesus. Amen."

The boys did not collect aluminum cans that week because T.J. and Aaron were both grounded. Every day after school, T.J. had to go to his room and stay there. He could only come out for dinner. Finally, the school week was over. Saturday rolled around and with it, a soccer game.

It was a beautiful fall day. T.J., Ricky, Zack, and Aaron sat in the back of T.J.'s family van. Sergeant, the family's German shepherd, sat with them. Sergeant loved soccer. He had quite a number of old soccer balls for himself in the backyard. He would chase them up and down the yard, dribbling with his nose. The boys had to keep a close eye on Sergeant or he would steal their good soccer balls.

The four boys chattered and laughed all the way to the soccer fields. It was especially fun for T.J. and Aaron. Although they had been allowed to go to soccer practice, they had been grounded from all other activities for a full week.

Upon arriving at the fields, the boys tumbled out of the van. They ran to find practice balls and began to warm up with their coach at one end of the field. The other team warmed up at the opposite end.

T.J. eyed the other team. The name of the other team was the Rockets. It was an older team, its members a full year older than the members on T.J.'s team.

"Aw, we'll beat 'em anyway," T.J. said to

himself, even though some of the boys on the Rockets team looked pretty big.

The referee signaled the start of the game. Aaron moved into the goal with Ricky as his right fullback. T.J. and Zack, as center forwards, hurried to the middle of the field. They would kick off for the Wildcats.

As T.J. positioned himself for the kickoff, he glanced across the circle at the members of the other team. His heart almost skipped a beat. There, a few feet away and staring right at him with an ugly scowl on his face, was Brandon Long, Ricky's next-door neighbor.

T.J. did not have time to think about Brandon, however. The whistle blew. Zack passed the ball to T.J. Faking a move around a Rockets player, T.J. dribbled the ball up the field. He then shot it over to Zack who was running squarely in line with T.J. and several yards to his left. In an excellent give-and-go play, Zack popped the ball back to T.J., who had sprinted up the field toward the goal. Without giving the Rockets fullbacks a chance to regroup, T.J. shot the ball into the right corner of the net. GOAL!

SHREEEE! went the referee's whistle. The crowd of parents on the Wildcats side of the field cheered loudly. Coach McLagan's voice could be heard above the rest.

"WAY TO GO, T.J. AND ZACK!"

The two boys grinned as they trotted back to the center line. They had moved quickly and scored within the first two minutes of the game against the team of older boys!

Getting into position and ready for the Rockets kickoff, T.J. found himself practically face-to-face with Brandon Long. When the whistle blew, Brandon ran full force into T.J., knocking him to the ground. There had been no reason for the knockdown. Brandon did not even have the ball in his possession.

SHREEEE! the referee called a foul on Brandon. Because of the foul, the ball went right back to the Wildcats.

Avoiding Brandon, T.J. ran ahead up the field while one of the halfbacks on his team kicked the ball. It was a perfect pass. The ball actually hit T.J. on the chest. T.J. got it under control and passed it over to Zack, who kicked it out to the right wing. The right wing dribbled the ball in a wide arc, and then shot it at the corner of the goal. It just missed going into the goal. The ball hit the right post and bounced to the center of the field. T.J. was ready for it, and headed the ball past the goalkeeper into the goal for the Wildcats' second goal of the game.

SHREEEE! the whistle announced the goal.

This time the parents really went wild.

"THAT'S USING YOUR HEAD, T.J.!" his father called out loudly.

T.J. grinned. He slapped his teammates' hands in victory as he trotted back to the center of the field. Maybe this would be a cinch. Maybe they were going to win easily against this older team.

That did not prove to be the case, however. The Rockets finally took possession of the ball and did not let go until they scored. Despite Ricky's brilliant defensive plays and Aaron's top-notch goalkeeping skills, the Rockets did score.

In the second quarter, the Wildcats scored once more, the goal going this time to Zack with T.J. getting the assist. The Rockets came back to score again on a long pass. It flew high above Ricky's head and just barely clipped the outstretched foot of a Rockets forward. He directed it past Aaron and into the net.

It was almost halftime. The score read Wildcats 3, Rockets 2. This time, the Rockets took possession of the ball. Brandon dribbled toward Aaron and the goal. Suddenly, Ricky charged out after him and tackled the ball so hard that Brandon fell flat on his face. He jumped up

immediately, and before Ricky had a chance to clear the ball out of his territory, Brandon jumped on Ricky and threw him to the ground. Aaron rushed out of the goal to help Ricky, but two other Rockets players grabbed Aaron and pushed him down.

Other members from both teams joined in the fight. T.J., watching from the other end of the field, could hardly believe it. He couldn't see Ricky, and that worried him. His sturdy Mexican friend had gone down under a pile of Rockets. Was he all right, or was he broken and bleeding under that pile?

6

DOGGY DISASTER

SHREEE! SHREEE! SHREEE! The referee blew on his whistle as he ran quickly to the pile of boys. T.J. ran after him. So did the coaches and linesmen.

The grown-ups pulled one boy after another out of the pile. Reaching the bottom, the referee yanked Brandon off of Ricky.

"Are you all right?" the referee asked Ricky.

"Yeah," Ricky slowly got up. "It would take more than that skinny Brandon to hurt me. After all, I'm a Rodriquez!"

T.J. smiled at his friend. He was glad Ricky was okay.

"Oh . . . oh," moaned Aaron, limping up beside T.J. and Ricky. He had been one of the boys on the bottom of the pile.

"Somebody smashed my foot!"

"It's a good thing it wasn't your head," said

Zack, coming to stand beside Aaron. The boys walked slowly off the field. They waited with their teammates to see what the referee's decision would be concerning the fight.

As it turned out, Brandon was suspended from the game. The other boys who had joined in the fight received official warnings. If they ever fought on the soccer field again, they would be suspended.

"But that's not fair!" Aaron told T.J. after he learned that an official warning would go down on his record. "I was just trying to help Ricky."

"I guess rules are rules," T.J. told his friend. "You broke the rules by fighting on the soccer field. Remember when we hid in the teachers' lounge? We were also trying to help Ricky. But we tried to do it the wrong way. You know what the police officer said. Even if you're trying to do something good, you have to follow the rules. If you break the rules, you must pay the penalty."

"Yeah, yeah," Aaron sighed. "I remember now. Maybe someday I'll learn."

"Learn what?" Zack asked.

"Learn not to help Ricky anymore," Aaron teased.

"Oh, you dope!" T.J. cried and playfully pushed Aaron to the ground.

The soccer game finally got under way again. After another three minutes, the game broke for halftime. In the second half of the game, T.J. and Zack picked up another goal apiece. Aaron played the game of his life, diving here and there for the ball, making blocks and saves at the net. But no one played the game any better than Ricky, the brown-skinned defender from Mexico. Not one of his opponents could shake him. Like a shadow, Ricky kept pace with them, following their every move, then suddenly attacking and winning the ball away. Several times, Ricky captured the ball and carried it all the way up the field before shooting it over to a forward on the team. In that way, Ricky scored two assists in the game.

The Wildcats went on to win the game, 7 to 5. Their parents cheered as the boys walked off the field. They had worked hard. They had won the battle against the older team.

On the way home, Mother said, "Ricky, I wish your father could have seen you play today. Your game was excellent!"

"Thank you," Ricky replied. "My whole family likes to watch the soccer games. Maybe someday they will be able to come to the games again."

"I'll tell you what we'll do," Father slapped his

hand on the steering wheel. "We will go inside and tell your family all about the game!"

And that's just what they did. When they got to Ricky's house, T.J.'s entire family went inside. Father recounted the game play by play to Ricky's father, who then translated for the other family members. It was a warm, happy time. It didn't matter that they were from different countries and different cultures, or that they did not speak each other's language. The two families formed special friendships that day. However, when Father told the part about the fight with Brandon, Ricky's father became very upset.

"Our neighbors do not give us a chance," he said sadly. "We have not done anything wrong to them. They hate us because we are Mexican!"

"I'm sorry," Father replied. "That's wrong. No one should judge people by the way they look or where they come from, but I'm afraid we have people in this country who do just that."

"It is not just in this country," Ricky's father shook his head. "There are prejudiced people in all countries, even Mexico."

"It's so sad," added Mother. "If people only knew how much they would gain by learning to be friends with all people everywhere."

"That is so right," the two men agreed.

The next Monday after school, T.J. officially began his aluminum can collection. He and Zack stood at the end of T.J.'s driveway with their dogs and wagons. They were waiting for Aaron.

"If he doesn't show up in the next five minutes, we're leaving without him," T.J. decided.

"Aw, he probably had to put a pink sweater on his poodle," laughed Zack.

"Yeah, or pink ribbons in her ears," T.J. chuckled.

"Or pink booties on her feet," added Zack.

The boys laughed hilariously. They petted their own dogs, thankful that they didn't have big white poodles. Sergeant, T.J.'s German shepherd, sat calmly in front of a wagon. T.J. had attached ropes to either side of Sergeant's harness and fastened the ropes to the wagon. Zack's golden retriever, Ranger, did not own a harness, so the boys had to rig one out of rope. Ranger did not like the makeshift harness and tried his best to chew through it.

"Ranger, cut it out!" Zack told his dog. Ranger had once again grabbed hold of the rope harness with his teeth. Zack pulled the rope out of Ranger's mouth.

"He's gonna bite through that harness," Zack warned T.J.

"Aw, that rope is really thick," T.J. replied. "Besides, once we get going, he won't have a chance to chew on it."

"If we ever get going," Zack grumbled.

"Where is that Aaron?" T.J. muttered. "Maybe I better go call him."

"Wait, I think I see him," Zack pointed down the street. "There he is!"

"Oh, no," T.J. groaned as Aaron came into view. "Look at that dog!"

Aaron's dog, Zsa Zsa, was already pulling a wagon. The large white poodle pranced skittishly in front of Aaron. She was dressed in a lavender sweater with pink hearts. Matching pink bows hung from her ears. But that wasn't all. Zsa Zsa wore a pink and white striped harness over her sweater!

"Here we are," announced the Wildcats' husky goalkeeper. He pulled Zsa Zsa to a stop right in front of Sergeant's nose. "Can you dig that crazy harness?" Aaron asked his friends. "I didn't even know Mom had it until today."

"I don't believe it," mumbled T.J. He sat down on the driveway and held his head in his hands.

"Aw, come on," Aaron poked T.J. with his foot. "You're just not used to high-class dogs," he teased. "See, Sergeant likes her already."

Indeed, the big German shepherd was busy sniffing Zsa Zsa's sweater and harness. He turned and gave T.J. a funny look as if to ask, "What kind of dog is this?"

The boys laughed. They got in a line and started off down the sidewalk. T.J. led the way with Sergeant. Aaron and Zsa Zsa came next. Zack and Ranger brought up the rear.

The boys stopped at every house along their route. They attracted much attention with their wagons and dogs, particularly Zsa Zsa. The boys soon learned that Zsa Zsa was an attention getter. People would come out of their houses to see the fancy-dressed poodle. That gave the boys a chance to tell them about their need for aluminum cans. Most everyone had cans to donate. One woman even supplied the dogs with dog biscuits.

Everything went fine for some time. The boys moved from house to house collecting soda pop cans. One man dumped a whole garbage bagful of cans into T.J.'s wagon.

"I was saving them to recycle myself," the man explained, "but it sounds like you have found a bigger need for them."

A woman gave them a box of cans, while another man donated three grocery sacks full!

The wagons were filling up fast. Soon the boys would have to return home to empty them. There were only three more houses on the block, so they decided to finish up that street and then start for home.

Just as they reached the last house, trouble began. A small black kitten darted off the porch and ran right under Zsa Zsa's nose. The high-strung poodle pulled the rope from Aaron's hand and whipped about so fast it looked like she had somersaulted in the air. The kitten ran out into the yard with Zsa Zsa in hot pursuit.

"STOP!" Aaron cried as he took out after Zsa

Zsa. The poodle's wagon bounced and jolted behind her. Cans flew in every direction.

The kitten, Zsa Zsa, and Aaron raced around the yard in circles. Finally, the kitten scrambled up a tall birch tree that sat off to one side of the yard. Zsa Zsa remained at the bottom of the tree whining and yapping at the top of her lungs.

"Zsa Zsa! You stupid dummy!" Aaron panted. It was no easy task to pull the poodle away from the tree. The dog, wagon, harness, and ropes were all tangled together.

T.J. and Zack laughed and laughed. They stopped quickly, however, when the front door of the house suddenly flew open and a voice cried, "What's going on out there?"

T.J. peered through the screen door. Behind it stood a short person with silvery white hair that stuck out wildly.

"Uh, one of our dogs chased your cat up a tree," T.J. answered rather nervously.

"Eh?" the person behind the screen door asked.

"One of our dogs has chased your cat up a tree," T.J. repeated loudly.

"Oh, dear!" The screen door opened and a little white-haired lady stepped out onto the porch. She was followed by a second little old lady, and then a third. The three women stood on the porch and blinked in amazement at what they saw. The yard was littered with aluminum cans and one overturned wagon. A noisy poodle in a pink and purple sweater barked continuously at the foot of the birch tree, while two big dogs with wagons lounged in the driveway.

"My goodness!" all three ladies exclaimed at once. They shaded their eyes and peered up at the top of the tree. There, in the uppermost branches perched the little black kitten.

"Oh, my! Penelope has never climbed a tree before," the first little old lady told T.J.

"Mark my words. She won't be able to make it down by herself," warned the second little old lady.

"Where is she?" cried the third little old lady. "I don't see her."

While the first two ladies tried to point out the kitten to the third lady, Aaron managed to get Zsa Zsa under control and away from the tree.

"The big bad dog is all gone now, Penelope," the first old lady called to the kitten. "You can come down now." The old lady hurried out into the yard to stand under the tree.

"She won't come down. She's too scared," declared the second old lady as she joined the first one under the tree.

"I still can't see her," the third old lady complained. "My eyes just can't focus that far."

"Never mind, Mathilda," the first old lady said to the third old lady. "Just help us try and call her down."

T.J., Zack, and Aaron watched as the three women stood under the tree and called, "Kitty, kitty, kitty!" over and over for several minutes. But no matter how much they called and coaxed, the kitten did not move. She clung to the top of the tree and cried, "Mew, mew, mew!"

"See, I told you she wouldn't come down on her own," said the second old lady. "She's too scared."

"Young man," the first old lady addressed T.J., "would you mind climbing the tree and rescuing our kitten?"

"Sure," T.J. answered eagerly. "No problem!"

Aaron and Zack gave T.J. a boost. He shinnied the rest of the way up the tall slender trunk to its lower branches. He then climbed branch by branch up the tree, although the branches were a bit far apart, and he had to stretch in a couple of places.

"Be careful!" the old ladies called up to him.

T.J. smiled to himself. He had not counted on

having to rescue a kitten from a tree, but the old ladies were nice, and he never minded a chance to climb an unfamiliar tree.

Plucking the kitten out of the branches was a different story, however. She had wrapped all four of her legs around a limb and was holding on tight. It took quite a bit of effort to free all four of her legs at once.

"Nice kitty. It's okay, kitty," T.J. stroked the kitten's fur, trying to calm her down. When he finally got her off the branch, he pushed the kitten down inside his jacket and started back down the tree.

"Mew, mew, mew," came the muffled voice of the kitten from inside T.J.'s jacket. Her soft, furry body was warm against his T-shirt. T.J. winced once or twice when the frightened kitten grabbed hold of his skin with her claws.

"Yay! Bravo!" everyone cried when T.J. and the kitten reached the ground.

"There, there, Penelope, it's all right," the three old ladies cooed and fussed over the kitten. They each had to have a turn holding her.

"Thank you, young man!" all three ladies called to T.J. They disappeared inside the house with Penelope.

The boys watched them go. They hadn't had a

chance to tell the old ladies why they had come to their house in the first place. T.J. shrugged and looked at his two friends. "They probably don't have any soda pop cans anyway. They probably only drink tea." All three of the boys laughed.

While T.J. was up in the tree, Zack and Aaron had picked up the cans in the yard. They had put all the cans back in Aaron's wagon and once more hooked Zsa Zsa to it.

"Let's go," T.J. said to his friends. With Zsa Zsa in tow, the boys turned to walk down the driveway to where they had left Sergeant and Ranger. When they turned, however, a surprise met their eyes. Sergeant and his wagon sat near the edge of the drive, Sergeant calmly licking one of his paws. But the place where Ranger had been sitting was now empty. Only the wagon and a few strands of rope remained nearby.

"OH, NO! RANGER'S GONE!" the boys cried at once.

7
EMERGENCY!

"I told you Ranger would chew through that rope harness," Zack told T.J. "Now look what's happened. He's gone!"

"Okay, okay, calm down. We'll find him," T.J. assured his friend. "Aaron, you stay here with Zsa Zsa and Sergeant and the wagons. Zack and I will go look for Ranger."

"Okay by me," Aaron replied and sprawled on the grass beside the old ladies' driveway.

Before starting off, T.J. and Zack scanned the area. They looked back the way they had come. There was no sign of Ranger that way, so the boys decided to cross the street and walk up another street that angled off in a different direction.

When they crossed the street, they caught a glimpse of two large golden retrievers playing inside a fenced-in yard. Neither boy paid any attention to the dogs, however, as they were inside a fence and seemed to belong there.

T.J. and Zack walked and walked up and down the neighborhood streets. They called Ranger's name over and over. Zack whistled his special call for Ranger. But nothing worked. The big yellow dog did not come to them. They could find no trace of him.

Tired and discouraged, T.J. and Zack returned to the old ladies' yard where Aaron was waiting for them. They sat down on the grass to rest.

"No luck, huh?" Aaron asked them.

T.J. shook his head.

"Oh, where could that dog have gone?" Zack moaned. "I gotta find him."

"Maybe he went home by himself," T.J. said. "Sometimes dogs do that, you know."

"Maybe," Zack replied glumly.

"Why don't we take the wagons and the other two dogs home?" T.J. suggested. "Then if Ranger's not there, we'll come back here and look for him again."

"Okay," Zack agreed. He sighed heavily. "I don't know what else to do."

The boys got to their feet, but just as they were ready to start for home, loud noises from across the street caught their attention.

"GET OUT OF MY YARD! SHOO!" cried a

woman's voice. "LEAVE MY DOG ALONE!"

As the astonished boys watched, a woman armed with a broom chased after one of the two golden retrievers that had been playing inside the fenced-in yard. As the big dog bounded over the fence, all three boys cried at once, "RANGER!"

The big yellow dog ran across the street and into Zack's open arms. Ranger got their faces wet as he gave all three boys wet, slobbery licks. The boys chattered and laughed.

"I can't believe he was right across the street all this time!" laughed T.J.

"Why didn't you come when I called, you big ninny?" Zack scolded the dog.

"Actually, I don't blame him a bit," remarked Aaron. "He probably decided that playing with another dog was much more fun than pulling a wagon full of cans."

T.J. and Zack laughed. They all got to their feet and started what seemed like a long walk home with three dogs and three wagons loaded down with aluminum cans. As they bumped and rattled along, T.J. felt tired but happy. They ought to get plenty of money for all these cans to help Ricky's family. That would make up for all the hassles of today.

"How much do you think we'll make on the

cans?" T.J. asked Zack and Aaron excitedly.

"Oh, maybe ten bucks," Zack replied.

"Ten bucks?" T.J. frowned. "I thought we'd make lots more. There are a lot of cans here."

"Well, maybe twenty bucks," Aaron offered.

"I was hoping for more like fifty," T.J. told them.

As soon as he got home, T.J. called the recycling center. He was terribly disappointed to learn just how little he would make on the cans.

"They're only gonna give me one penny a can," T.J. complained to Father and Mother at dinnertime. "I counted all the cans we got today and there are 253 cans. So, that means I get 253 cents, which is only $2.53. That's not enough money to help Ricky's family."

"Aren't you going to keep on collecting cans?" asked Father.

"Well, yeah, but at that rate, it'll take us forever to make enough money to help Ricky's family," T.J. scowled.

"Two dollars and fifty-three cents a day isn't so bad," said Mother.

"It isn't so good either," T.J. replied glumly. "It's like I said before. A kid can't really do anything big to help people out."

"That's not completely true," Mother said. "I

can think of a specific instance when Jesus used a kid to bring about a mighty big miracle."

"What was that?" T.J. wanted to know.

"One day when Jesus had preached to a crowd of people for a long time, He noticed that they were tired and hungry. They were way out in the countryside with no grocery stores available. There was only one person who had any food—a little boy. He had a lunch that his mother had packed for him. In his lunch sack were two small fish and five small loaves of bread. That was all. Surely that was not enough to feed a crowd of people, do you think?" Mother asked.

"No way," said T.J.

"Well, Jesus must have thought it was, because He took that little boy's lunch and began breaking it into pieces and passing it out to the crowd. And what do you think happened?" asked Mother.

"You mean He fed all those people with that little bit of food?" T.J. asked in amazement.

"That's right," Mother smiled. "The fish and the bread kept multiplying right before their eyes. He ended up with enough food to feed five thousand men and their families! There was even food left over!"

"Wow!" T.J. breathed. "I bet that boy thought

that was totally cool."

"So you see," Mother went on, "it doesn't matter how small you are or how little you have. If you give what you can, God will multiply it and make it be enough."

"Do you think God would multiply the cans for me?" T.J. asked excitedly.

"I think that if you ask Him, God will make your aluminum can collection turn out just the way it should," Mother answered. "I don't know what method He might use, but I know He will help you if you ask."

"All right!" T.J. said. He felt better now. He thought for a moment and then said to his father, "Dad, would you multiply the money I get for the cans just like God multiplied the fish and the bread for Jesus?"

Father laughed. "I don't think I can multiply it by five thousand like God did, but I'll tell you what I'll do."

"What?" T.J. asked eagerly.

"I'll multiply the money you get for the cans by two," Father promised. "That means I'll double it."

"Okay," T.J. agreed. Things were looking up. Now all he had to do was get as many cans as he possibly could.

That night, T.J. said in his prayers, "Dear Father in heaven, please help me collect a whole bunch of cans. Please multiply them like You multiplied the fish and the bread for Jesus. I pray in Jesus' name. Amen."

All that week and the next, T.J. and his friends scoured the neighborhood for aluminum soda pop cans. There was not one neighbor in the multiblock area whom the boys did not visit. Father brought home cans from the office. So did Zack's and Aaron's fathers. Mother helped the boys pick up cans from doctors' and dentists' offices and from various local businesses in the surrounding areas. Even Mrs. Larson let the boys have all the soda pop cans from the teachers' lounge. Of course, they had to collect them after school.

The result was amazing. T.J. could not believe the number of calls he received each day to pick up cans from different locations. The word had spread rapidly from neighbor to neighbor and from business to business.

"This is incredible!" Father exclaimed one evening to Mother and T.J. He had helped them load boxes and sacks full of empty cans into the family van to haul to the recycling center the next day. The van was so full of cans that there was only room enough for the driver and one passenger.

"This is a full-blown miracle," Mother decided. "Only God could pull this one off."

"When I asked God to multiply the cans, I didn't know He would give me this many," T.J. told his parents.

"How much money have you made so far on these cans?" Father asked T.J.

"Forty-two dollars," T.J. replied.

"Wow!" Father exclaimed. "That's more than four thousand cans!"

"We have collected at least that many more," Mother said. "I have never seen the van so tightly packed."

"Looks like you are going to have lots of money to give to Ricky's family," Father told T.J.

"Yeah, Dad, and remember, you are going to multiply the money," T.J. reminded his father.

"When I promised to do that I sure didn't know what I was getting myself into, did I?" Father laughed. He gave T.J a squeeze and then joined him in a playful wrestling match.

One day after school, T.J. walked home with Ricky. T.J. had been invited to dinner at Ricky's house that evening. He looked forward to having a real honest-to-goodness Mexican meal.

When they reached Ricky's house, the two boys spent some time in the yard playing on the tree swing. Soon, however, the sky became quite dark. Thunder began to rumble, first in the distance, but it quickly got louder and louder. Big drops of rain began to fall. The boys ran inside and watched the storm from the big picture window in Ricky's living room.

"Wow! This is a big storm," T.J. remarked. He loved to watch thunderstorms. "Hey, did you see that lightning bolt?"

"Yeah," said Ricky. "If there's lightning, I'm glad I'm not out there."

"Me, too," T.J. agreed. He stared out the window. "Hey, there is someone out there. See? Over there by the street. Somebody's hopping up and down. You can just barely see him." T.J. pointed out the window to the left side of the yard.

"Oh," Ricky squinted through the glass. "It looks like my creepy neighbor, Brandon. That doesn't surprise me. He's always doing something weird."

"But what could he be doing out in the rain?" T.J. wanted to know.

"Who cares?" Ricky turned away from the window. "I don't want to look at Brandon. Let's play a game instead." He got out a board game, but before he could set it up, a loud POP! and CRACKLE! sounded outside, and the lights went off. The house was plunged into semidarkness.

Somewhere in a back bedroom, a child began to cry. A torrent of Spanish words flowed from the kitchen.

"My mother put dinner in the oven to bake right before the electricity went off. Now she says the oven won't work," Ricky translated for T.J.

Ricky's father brought a candle on a stand into

the living room. He lit it. Its soft glow helped to lighten the darkness of the room.

"The electricity better go on soon, or we will be eating cold tamale pie," Ricky's father told the boys with a smile.

T.J. sat on the floor, his arms wrapped around his knees, and stared at the warm glow of the candle. It seemed so peaceful compared to the raging storm outside. The candle made T.J. feel safe and warm. He didn't care if the electricity never came back on.

T.J.'s peaceful feeling ended abruptly, however. A loud banging on the front door brought the boys and Ricky's father quickly to their feet. Opening the door, Ricky's father pulled a drenched figure into the room. Ricky and T.J. gasped in surprise. It was Brandon!

"PLEASE HELP ME!" Brandon cried. "MY LITTLE BROTHER IS CAUGHT IN THE RAIN GUTTER BELOW THE STREET! I THINK HE IS GOING TO DROWN!"

8
MULTIPLE MIRACLES

Ricky's father did not waste time. He pulled on a rain jacket and followed Brandon out of the door. Ricky and T.J. threw on their jackets and hurried out into the storm. They wanted to be part of the action.

By the time he crossed the front yard, T.J. was soaked from head to toe. His jacket and shoes could not keep out the heavy downpour. Water flowed from his hair down his neck. It was as if he were in the shower. But none of that mattered as T.J. looked with frightened eyes at the scene in front of him.

Brandon and Mr. Rodriquez stared down through a raised gutter opening at the side of the street. It led to the sewer pipes that ran underground. T.J. moved up closer to get a better look. He could barely glimpse the figure of a boy, no older than his own seven-year-old brother, hanging on for dear life to a narrow metal bar that spanned the width of the gutter opening. Water from the sewer swirled below him. Rainwater from the gutter splashed over his head as it rushed through the gutter opening to the sewer below.

"HELP!" the boy cried over and over. Although his eyes were closed tight, his face was a mask of panic and terror. He could not let go, or he would fall into the swirling water below and be washed through the pipes.

"How did he get in there?" T.J. asked in amazement. He surely hadn't crawled through the gutter opening from the street. It was only a few inches wide.

"We were crawling through the sewer pipes down under the street," Brandon explained. "You can get to them from the creek that runs behind our house. I got out okay but my brother, Stephen, got scared and wouldn't follow me back out through the pipes. Then the rain came and he got caught in the water. Somehow he was able to climb up as high as the street opening."

T.J. and Ricky stared at one another in disbelief. How could anyone be so stupid as to crawl through sewer pipes? Besides being filthy and unsanitary, they were extremely dangerous, as Brandon and his brother had found out the hard way.

Ricky's father did not wait to hear any more. "Talk to your brother," he told Brandon. "Tell him to hang on. We're going to get him out. I have to go get some tools." With that, Mr. Rodriquez ran back across the yard and into the house.

"Hold on, Stephen!" Brandon shouted in his brother's ear. "Help is here. We're going to get you out."

"I can't . . . hold on . . . " Stephen gasped. He had stopped screaming. He looked completely worn out, as if he had used the last of his strength.

"Oh, don't let go!" T.J. shouted and moved to join Brandon in front of the gutter opening. He got down on his hands and knees to talk to the younger boy. Ricky did the same.

"Don't worry!" Ricky called to Stephen. "My dad's going to rescue you. He's coming right back with some tools. He knows what to do."

"Yeah, just hold on for another minute," T.J. tried to encourage Stephen. "We'll have you out of there right away."

Brandon looked gratefully at Ricky and T.J. He sank down on the pavement. He seemed half-drowned himself.

Ricky's father returned quickly. He carried a box of tools and some rope. Squatting down beside the manhole cover on top of the gutter, he used a hammer and crowbar to loosen and raise the heavy iron cover. It took a good deal of strength to remove it and slide it off of the opening.

Without hesitation, Ricky's father climbed down the slippery, wet iron rungs fastened in concrete at the back of the gutter. Holding onto one of the rungs, he tried to reach Stephen, but the boy was too high and far away from the rungs.

Climbing back up the rungs, Mr. Rodriquez grabbed the rope. Shouting against the roar of water, he called to the boys, "I'm going back down in there. Be ready to help Stephen out of the manhole. I'll push him up to you."

"Dad, be careful!" Ricky shouted in alarm.

"Don't worry," his father replied, "just pray for me and Stephen." He hurriedly tied one end of the rope around his waist. The other end he fastened to the top rung and climbed back down inside the manhole.

Watching through the gutter opening and praying fervently, T.J. watched Mr. Rodriquez jump from the bottom rung to the floor of the sewer. The area in which he stood was a narrow rectangular space filled in with concrete. A large sewer pipe opened into it from the back of the gutter. Mr. Rodriquez stood in knee-deep water that swirled and churned around him. He positioned himself directly under Stephen. Reaching up as high as he could, Ricky's father grabbed hold of Stephen's legs, just above his knees.

"LET GO OF THE BAR!" Mr. Rodriquez called to Stephen. "I'LL CATCH YOU!"

Stephen hesitated for a moment. He had been holding on so tightly for so long that it was very hard to let go.

"It's okay," Ricky told Stephen. "My dad's really strong. He will catch you."

Stephen did not wait any longer. He let go of the bar at the top of the gutter and fell backward into Mr. Rodriquez's arms.

Ricky's father held Stephen for a minute or two to calm the little boy. He then tucked Stephen under his left arm and made the short hop back to the rungs that provided the only way out of the manhole.

Climbing with one arm, Ricky's father pushed Stephen ahead of him up the rungs and out of the manhole. Brandon, T.J., and Ricky grabbed hold of Stephen and pulled him to safety. They then helped Ricky's father out of the hole.

Mr. Rodriquez untied the rope from the top rung and pushed the heavy cover back in place on top of the manhole. CLANG! Metal upon metal banged as it dropped into place.

"Come inside our house," Ricky's father shouted to Brandon. Mr. Rodriquez carried Stephen across the yard and into the house. The boys followed and once inside the house, Ricky's parents gave Stephen dry clothes. His brother helped him change, then they wrapped him in two blankets. The electricity was still off, but Mrs. Rodriquez had built a fire in the fireplace. Stephen was set in a chair by the fire. Mrs. Rodriquez pulled out a blackened coffeepot from among the fire embers. From it, she poured steaming hot water into a mug. She made some weak tea and gave it to Stephen to drink.

The other boys went to Ricky's room to change their wet clothes. Ricky gave them each warm sweatshirts, pants, and socks, although Ricky's jeans were a bit too short for Brandon.

"Just pull your socks up high," Ricky told Brandon. The boys chuckled.

The boys returned to the living room, and everyone sat down to rest. Soon, the color returned to Stephen's face. The tea and warm fire seemed to be helping.

"Where are your parents?" Ricky's father asked Brandon.

"They are still at work," Brandon said. "They

own the Best Seller Bookstore at the Kingswood Shopping Mall. They have to stay at the store until it closes."

Ricky's father translated what Brandon had said to Ricky's mother. She answered back in Spanish.

"My wife says you must eat dinner here with us. We also ought to call your parents and tell them what has happened."

"Yeah," Brandon agreed. He gazed at Mr. Rodriquez with a grateful face. "Thank you for rescuing my brother."

"You're welcome," Ricky's father replied.

Brandon turned to Ricky and T.J. "I'm really sorry for calling you names and fighting and stuff. I guess I've been a real jerk." Brandon looked down at the floor in embarrassment.

"It's okay," Ricky and T.J. told him.

"I just hope we can all be friends now," Mr. Rodriquez said to Brandon.

"You can count on it," Brandon smiled.

"Let's go call your parents," suggested Mr. Rodriquez. He got up to lead Brandon to the kitchen telephone. Just at that moment, the lights in the room flickered on.

"Yea!" everyone cried. The electricity had returned. Mrs. Rodriquez hurried into the kitchen to see about dinner. Mr. Rodriquez and Brandon went to use the telephone. T.J. and Ricky stayed behind with Stephen. They looked at one another and smiled. Things had worked out wonderfully. They had rescued Stephen, and Brandon was now their friend. T.J. sighed happily. Who would have believed things would turn out this way? Only God could have made it possible. Here was another miracle.

The next day, Ricky came to school all excited. "You won't believe it! The most exciting thing has happened!"

"What?" T.J. wanted to know.

"My dad has a job!" Ricky said with a grin.

"Wow!" cried T.J. "How'd that happen?"

"Well, it's really kinda funny. Wait 'til you hear about it," Ricky told him. "Last night, after you went home, Brandon and Stephen's parents came over. They were really grateful to my dad for rescuing Stephen. They started talking and found out that my dad was out of work. So they gave him a job! He's going to work at their bookstore. Isn't that funny? They used to hate us, but now they like us so much that they want my dad to work for them!"

"That is funny," T.J. agreed.

When T.J. told his parents about it that evening, Father and Mother were amazed.

"I think God is performing all kinds of miracles right now, T.J.," Father declared.

"Yeah, I do too," T.J. said excitedly. "He multiplied the cans. He helped Mr. Rodriquez rescue Stephen. He helped Brandon and his parents become friends with Ricky's family, and now He even gave Ricky's dad a job!"

"That is a major miracle considering Ricky's dad and Brandon's family were former enemies," remarked Mother.

"Yeah," T.J. suddenly frowned. "What about the can money now? Since Mr. Rodriquez has a job, maybe he won't need it."

"Oh, I'm sure he'll need it," Father assured T.J. "After all, Mr. Rodriquez won't get his first paycheck right away. He will still have to buy food for that big family. He may have some bills that he hasn't been able to pay. Your can money will be a big blessing to him."

"That's right," said Mother. "I think this is God's way of telling you that it is now time to end the can collection and give the money to the Rodriquezes."

"Yeah," T.J. thought it over. "That sounds right to me. Since tomorrow's Saturday, we can take the rest of the cans to the recycling center and then go give the money to Ricky's family."

"Good idea," Father agreed. "Aren't you forgetting one thing?" he asked T.J.

"What?"

"You didn't mention that your father needs to know the total amount of money you get for the cans so that he can double it," replied Father with a wink.

"Oh, don't worry, Dad," T.J. replied. "I won't forget that."

They all laughed.

Even though the next day was Saturday, T.J. got up early. He was excited. He had been waiting for this day to come for a long time. This was the day he would give the money to the Rodriquez family.

Mother and Father helped T.J. load the last of the aluminum cans into the van. Father took T.J. to the recycling center and then to the bank, while Mother took Charley and the girls to Charley's early morning soccer game. T.J. also had a Saturday soccer game, but it wasn't until that afternoon.

At the bank, T.J. handed over all of the money to a teller. She counted it carefully.

"That's $144.28," the teller said.

"My goodness!" Father acted shocked. "You mean I have to double that much money?"

T.J. began to laugh. "You promised!"

The teller looked confused. Father explained the situation to her. She looked at T.J. and said, "You mean you're the boy who has been picking up the aluminum cans from the bank every week?"

T.J. nodded. He was a bit embarrassed as people were staring at him.

"Oh, look everybody!" the teller called loudly to the other employees of the bank. "Here's the boy who's been collecting all the cans. He's going to give the money to the needy family today."

Several bank employees came over to shake T.J.'s hand. T.J. felt his ears turn red as they all made a fuss over him. But the biggest surprise was yet to come. The bank president came out of his office to meet T.J. He had someone take T.J.'s picture.

"We're going to write an article about you for our next bank newsletter," the president told T.J. He gave T.J. a big box of candy, a new blanket, and a popcorn popper, all to go to the Rodriquez family. They were gifts the bank gave away to new customers.

"Wow!" was all T.J. could say. He was completely overwhelmed.

Father doubled the money and had the teller make out a bank check to the Rodriquez family for $288.56. They thanked everyone at the bank and carried the presents and the check out to the van. Sitting inside the van, Father paused and looked at T.J.

"I'd say God is still working for us, wouldn't you?" he asked T.J.

T.J. nodded. "He's still multiplying!"

Father and T.J. met Mother and the other children at a restaurant for lunch. When Mother saw all the presents from the bank, tears filled her eyes.

"God is so good!" she exclaimed. "We need to thank Him."

They said a thank-you prayer to God, and then ate a quick lunch. Before going to Ricky's house, they returned home to get T.J.'s soccer clothes and to pick up Zack and Aaron.

When they reached the Rodriquez house, T.J., Zack, and Aaron walked to the door in front of the others. T.J. carried the check and the box of candy. Zack carried the blanket, and Aaron carried the popcorn popper.

Ricky answered the door. His eyes opened wide when he saw the Fairbanks family and the three boys loaded down with gifts.

"Come in," he cried and called for his parents. Ricky's parents and grandparents hurried into the living room.

"What's all this?" Ricky's father asked in amazement.

For a moment, there was an awkward silence. Everyone looked at T.J. He stepped forward and handed the check to Mr. Rodriquez.

"Zack and Aaron and I have been collecting aluminum cans and getting money for them at the recycling center," he told Ricky's father. "We did it for you and your family. Since you were out of work, we wanted you to have the money."

For a moment, Mr. Rodriquez said nothing. He looked like he wanted to speak but couldn't. Finally, he grabbed T.J. and hugged him tight. He then hugged the other boys. Tears were in his eyes as he spoke in Spanish to his family. He passed the check around so everyone could see it. They all began talking at once. Mrs. Rodriquez burst into tears and ran from the room. She soon returned with a big smile on her face.

"This money is a gift from God," Mr. Rodriquez told the boys. "We were down to our very last dollar. Now we will have enough to live on until I get my first paycheck. I and my family thank you."

"You're welcome," T.J. smiled. "This is for you too." He handed Ricky's father the box of candy.

"Don't tell me this is from the recycling center too?" Mr. Rodriquez laughed.

"No, it's from the bank," T.J. replied. He and Father told everyone about their experience at the bank.

Zack gave Mr. Rodriquez the blanket. Aaron handed the popcorn popper to Ricky's mother.

"I wish this was cookie baking sheets," Aaron told her. "Then you could make even more of those famous cinnamon sugar cookies!" Aaron rubbed his stomach.

Ricky translated for his mother. She laughed and ran to the kitchen. When she returned, she carried a big platterful of her famous cookies.

The two families and friends sat in the Rodriquez living room and talked and laughed together. Charley, Megan, and Elizabeth made immediate friends with Ricky's younger brothers and sisters.

"Hey, maybe now your family can go watch the soccer games," T.J. said to Ricky as the boys sat in the middle of the floor munching on cookies.

Ricky quickly turned and asked his father if he could bring the family to the soccer game that afternoon.

"The soccer game!" Father and Mother suddenly cried in alarm. They had forgotten all about it.

Everyone rushed around and got ready to go. Both families went to the game. As T.J. rode in the back of the van with his friends, he could not keep from grinning. Everything had gone so well—even better than he had hoped. He knew God was responsible. His mother was right. God is so good!

Amen.